P9-BII-879

THE WORLD OF MARTIAL ARTS

MASTERS & HEROES

BY JIM OLLHOFF

Visit us at
www.abdopublishing.com

Published by ABDO Publishing Company, 8000 West 78th Street, Suite 310, Edina, MN 55439.
Copyright ©2008 by Abdo Consulting Group, Inc. International copyrights reserved in all countries.
No part of this book may be reproduced in any form without written permission from the publisher.
ABDO & Daughters™ is a trademark and logo of ABDO Publishing Company.

Printed in the United States.

Editor: John Hamilton
Graphic Design: John Hamilton
Cover Design: Neil Klinepier
Cover Illustration: Corbis
Interior Photos and Illustrations: p 4 monk at Shaolin Temple, Getty Images; p 6 (top left) tiger, Getty Images; (top right) boy posing in tiger stance, Getty Images; p 9 Miyamoto Musashi, Corbis; p 10 Musashi in dueling hall, Corbis; p 11 man dressed as samurai, Corbis; p 12 map of Okinawa, U.S. Central Intelligence Agency; p 13 swordsman on sandy beach, Getty Images; p 15 Asian bull, iStockphoto; p 17 man shows bo technique to class of students, Getty Images; p 19 man dressed as samurai, Corbis; p 20 boy performs up-block, iStockphoto; p 21 man practicing kicks, Corbis; p 23 man in white uniform performs punch, Getty Images; p 25 torso and hands of karate practitioner, Getty Images; p 27 black belt student stands in dojo, Getty Images; p 28 pair of karate stylists practice stances, Getty Images; p 29 gold belt students bow to each other, Corbis.

Library of Congress Cataloging-in-Publication Data

Ollhoff, Jim, 1959-
  Masters & heroes / Jim Ollhoff.
    p. cm. -- (The world of martial arts)
  Includes index.
  ISBN 978-1-59928-981-6
  1. Martial artists--Biography--Juvenile literature. I. Title. II. Title: Masters and heroes.

GV1113.A2O55 2008
796.80922--dc22
  [B]
                            2007030551

武道

CONTENTS

BODHIDHARMA: DID HE START IT ALL?

Facing Page:
A portrait of Bodhidharma.
Below: A monk practices kung fu at the main gate to China's Shaolin Temple.

One of the great questions in martial arts is, "Who started it all?" One legend says that a Buddhist monk named Bodhidharma started the martial arts sometime around 500 A.D. It is only a legend, but people have told stories about Bodhidharma for centuries.

Bodhidharma was a monk from southern India. One day he decided to travel to China. He walked northward for months, through forests, swamps, and over mountains, until he finally arrived at his destination. He went to a Buddhist monastery in central China. Tucked away in a green forest, this monastery was called *Shaolin,* which means "young forest." Bodhidharma taught the monks about Zen, a type of meditation that requires sitting for a long time.

Above: Popular legend says that the foundation of kung fu is based on the movements of animals. In the photo at top right, a young kung fu stylist poses in a tiger stance.

Bodhidharma tried to teach the students about Zen, but they were not physically fit. They were inactive, and would frequently fall asleep while they were meditating. They were so unhealthy that Bodhidharma knew they could never learn anything until they became stronger and more fit. He knew he would need to teach them how to exercise. When the monks were more physically fit, they would be able to meditate for longer periods.

Bodhidharma wondered what kind of exercises would help the monks. He looked to nature for clues. He watched how animals move, and created a series of exercises based on those movements. Bodhidharma taught the monks how to move like a tiger, a monkey, a crane, or a praying mantis. The monks practiced these movements and eventually became physically fit. Not only that, Bodhidharma realized that the monks knew how to defend themselves when they got into fights or were attacked by bandits. The monks used the same kinds of defensive techniques that animals used.

As the years went by, the Shaolin monks began using techniques that were more and more effective. They refined their fighting methods but continued to copy animal movements. Today, many kung fu styles and movements have animal names, like "the lion chases its tail," or "eagle spreads its wings."

There are other fantastic stories and legends told of Bodhidharma. One story says he was meditating one day and fell asleep. When he awoke, he

was so angry with himself for falling asleep that he cut off his own eyelids so that he would never sleep again. He then planted his own eyelids in the ground, which caused the first tea plant to sprout. Another story says Bodhidharma once meditated facing a wall for nine years without eating, drinking, or talking to another person.

Above: A painting of Bodhidharma meditating in a cave.

The idea that Bodhidharma created the martial arts is a popular story, but it probably isn't true. Historians disagree on whether or not there was such a person as Bodhidharma. The legend began with a story that is only a few hundred years old. Did Bodhidharma really begin the martial arts? It is more likely that martial arts emerged in many different places at many times. Still, the idea that one man began all the martial arts in the world is a popular one.

Miyamoto Musashi: The Great Swordsman

Miyamoto Musashi (1584?-1645) is considered by many to be the greatest swordsman of all time. He was a *ronin*, a samurai without a master. He wandered Japan looking for duels, and later sought enlightenment.

When Musashi was born, Japan was not under the rule of one central government. It was a violent place, with wars and battles happening constantly. Duels, challenges, and matches to the death were a daily occurrence.

Musashi learned sword-fighting skills at an early age because his father was a samurai and a martial artist. According to legend, Musashi fought his first sword duel when he was just 13. By age 15 or 16, he had left home and was traveling the countryside, engaging in duels. Swordsmen who wanted to show everyone how good they were would post a challenge in the village, saying they would fight anyone who dared. Musashi was eager to accept these challenges. He always won. Musashi says in his later writings that he fought more than 60 duels, and won them all. Mortal combat was a way of life at this time in Japan.

Above: A self-portrait of Miyamoto Musashi, Japan's greatest swordsman.

Above: Miyamoto Musashi defeats four opponents in a dueling hall. In the hands of the master swordsman, even wooden practice swords were lethal weapons.

Musashi probably fought in the famous Battle of Sekigahara in 1600, at the age of 16. He fought on the losing side, but he survived and escaped.

Musashi continued wandering the countryside. By the time he was in his early 20s, he had stopped using a sword. Winning duels had become too easy. To challenge himself, he began using only a wooden staff in the shape of a sword.

Over the next few decades, Musashi served various rulers. He opened a school for sword fighting. He studied Confucianism, Buddhism, and Taoism. By the time he was in his late 40s, he was studying painting and sculpture. When he was 60, he went to live by himself high in the mountains. There, he wrote books on strategy and life. He looked back on his wild youth, thinking that he may have won many battles by luck.

Left: A Japanese man from the late 1800s dressed in armor and holding a katana, or samurai sword.

Musashi believed that samurai must be good at many things, not just swordplay. He said, "To learn the sword, study the guitar. To learn unarmed fighting, learn commerce." He believed that if people only studied one thing, it would make them narrow and vulnerable, and prevent them from growth. In his later years, he became an accomplished artist, sculptor, and calligrapher.

One of Musashi's most famous mottoes was, "The true martial artist should be well versed in the art of the pen as well as the sword."

Musashi died at age 61, probably of cancer. Today, people regard him as the *Kensei*, or sword saint, of Japan.

Okinawan Masters: Life Lessons Through Karate

Many cultures of the world use stories as a way to tell important truths. Karate instructors from Okinawa, which is today situated in southern Japan, have done this very thing. They tell stories about the great karate masters, relating episodes from their lives in ways that make important points about the martial art of karate.

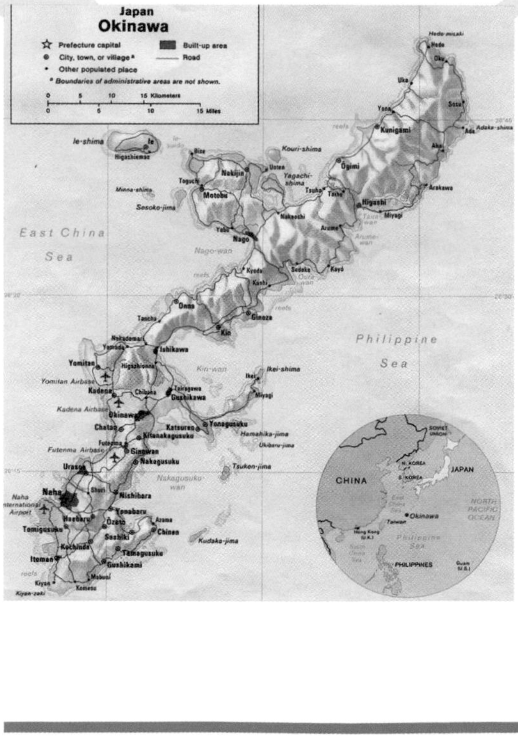

The stories have been told for many years, from generation to generation, so they may not be historically accurate. Sometimes the stories take on new details with each retelling. However, the point of the stories remains the same—to teach us something about karate, and perhaps life.

Japan
Okinawa

☆ Prefecture capital   ▪ Built-up area
● City, town, or village ▪   —— Road
▪ Other populated place
* Boundaries of administrative areas are not shown.

East China Sea

Philippine Sea

CHINA   JAPAN

Above: By reading stories about the old karate masters, we can learn much about both the martial arts and life.

MASTER BUSHI MATSUMURA

Above: A portrait of karate master Bushi Matsumura.

In the early 1800s, there lived a great karate master named Bushi Matsumura. The king of Okinawa at that time was a corrupt ruler who charged very high taxes. He used the tax money to live a life of luxury, instead of using it to help his own people.

The Okinawan king knew the people were angry about the high taxes, so he gave them something else to occupy their thoughts. He distracted them with a bullfight, pitting a prize bull from Japan against the greatest karate master in Okinawa, Bushi Matsumura. The announcement of the unusual event spread all over the island, and everyone was very excited.

Bushi didn't want to fight the bull. But the king had ordered him to fight, so he had little choice. In the middle of the night, two weeks before the event, Bushi went to the pen where the bull was kept. Bushi entered the pen. The bull was angry and tried to charge Bushi. The karate master pulled a long needle from his sleeve and poked the bull in the nose with the needle. Every night for the next two weeks, Bushi went into the pen and poked the bull in the nose with the long needle.

When the day came for the fight, huge crowds gathered. The bull charged into the ring, pawing at the ground and

snorting angrily. Everyone was cheering and excited, but wondered if even the great Bushi Matsumura could handle this bull. Finally, Bushi appeared. He slowly entered the ring. The bull snorted ferociously, and got ready to charge him. Bushi walked calmly toward the bull. Suddenly, the bull smelled Bushi and realized who he was. The bull bellowed and ran away from Bushi, cowering on the other side of the ring. The crowds went wild—Bushi had defeated the bull without lifting a finger.

Karate instructors sometimes tell this story to remind students that karate is not just about fast kicks and strong punches. Karate students must use their brains as well.

Above: When Bushi Matsumura defeated the bull, he proved that karate masters must use their brains as well as their muscles.

MASTER KYAN CHOTOKU

Above: Okinawan karate master Kyan Chotoku.

There was a time when the road between two major Okinawan cities, Naha and Shuri, was under the control of gangs. These criminals would rob people who were traveling after sundown along the road. The problem grew worse and worse. Even the police seemed powerless to stop the hoodlums.

Finally, the townspeople called the great karate master Kyan Chotoku, a former student of Bushi Matsumura, to see if there was anything he could do. He agreed to help the people.

Every night, Kyan walked the road, singing loudly and carrying a chicken under each arm. He was trying to attract the hoodlums. Finally, one night, four young men jumped out and stopped him. Three stood in front of Kyan, and one behind. One of the thugs had a sword. "Stop!" they commanded menacingly. "Give us your money!"

Kyan responded calmly, "I have just bought these two chickens. My mother is sick and I'm going to make chicken soup for her."

"Do you think we're joking?" said the thug with the sword. "Give us your money or you die!" Kyan remained calm, which made the hooligans more nervous.

Kyan replied, "Well, I have a little bit of change from the purchase of the chickens. I suppose I could give that to you." Still holding the chickens, Kyan reached into his pocket, pulled out some change, and gave it to the robbers. He then started to walk on, but they blocked his way.

"Wait," the robbers said, "we want the chickens, too." Kyan sighed. "Oh, all right," he said. Kyan flung the chickens toward their heads and simultaneously poked the eye of one of the thugs. With his other hand he struck a second thug in the throat. Like lightning, Kyan then kicked another bandit in the midsection, dropping him instantly. He whirled on the man behind him, who recoiled in fear and ran away.

Kyan turned back to the thugs writhing in pain on the ground. Kyan told them, "You are hurting society with your lawlessness. Today was only a lesson in manners. Next time, it will mean your death." After that night, the street between Shuri and Naha became safe again.

This story reminds us that the purpose of karate is to help and protect people, not to cause injury or mayhem.

Above: A good instructor teaches students not just about martial arts, but also important lessons in how to help others.

Master Itoman Bunkichi

In the mid-1800s, Okinawa sometimes had to deal with rogue Japanese samurai. Japanese leaders expelled these samurai, and now these men were looking for trouble. Itoman Bunkichi was a great karate master, known for his agility and jumping ability.

One day, Itoman stood on a bridge talking with a female friend. A disgruntled samurai approached, wanting to pick a fight with someone. The samurai began hurling insults at the Okinawan. Itoman pretended not to hear, and continued to talk to the woman. Infuriated, the samurai lunged at Itoman to knock him down. However, Itoman shifted his body just as the samurai lunged. The samurai fell flat on his face.

Itoman continued talking to his friend as if the samurai were not even there. This made the samurai even madder. He got up and charged Itoman again. Once more, without even losing eye contact with his friend, Itoman shifted his weight. The samurai grabbed only empty air. Now the samurai was humiliated as well as angry.

The samurai drew his sword. "I'm going to teach you a lesson!" he cried, charging forward and swinging his sword. Itoman easily avoided the sword thrust, and then simply leapt over the railing of the bridge.

Above: A reenactor dressed as a Japanese samurai.

Above: Years of martial arts training brings confidence in one's abilities. Oftentimes, martial artists learn that violence is not necessary to diffuse conflicts.

The samurai stopped. He was a little confused because he had not heard a splash. The samurai peered over the railing, trying to understand where Itoman had gone. He peered further over the railing. Then he leaned even further.

Itoman had jumped over the railing and grabbed the supports under the bridge. Swinging like a monkey under the bridge, he had climbed up the other side, behind the samurai. Itoman grabbed the samurai from behind and pushed him over the railing into the river. Without using his karate skills, Itoman had defeated the samurai.

In Okinawan karate, one of the most important philosophies is that there is no first attack in karate. That means that karate skills must never be used for attacking, only for defense of others or ourselves. Any person who is the first one to attack dishonors karate.

Above: U.S. Army specialist Kenneth Christensen practices karate as the sun sets in the desert outside Kuwait City, Kuwait.

Gichin Funakoshi: Bringing Martial Arts to the World

Above: Gichin Funakoshi.

Gichin Funakoshi (1868-1957) is often called the father of modern karate. Through his efforts, karate became popular in Japan and the United States. He dedicated his life to bringing karate to the world.

Funakoshi was born in the town of Shuri, on the island of Okinawa, in 1868. The Japanese government controlled Okinawa at that time. In Japan, momentous changes were occurring. In the same year Funakoshi was born, Japan began the Meiji Restoration. This was the end of the feudal period in Japan. The samurai class had been disbanded, and efforts to modernize Japan went into full swing.

Practicing karate was against the law in those days. Nevertheless, at the age of 16, Funakoshi found a karate master named Yasutsune Azato, and began to study with him.

Above: A man practices shotokan karate, a style founded by Gichin Funakoshi.

Funakoshi lived with his grandparents at the time, and Azato's house was a few miles away. Because the practice of karate was against the law, Funakoshi had to study at night. So, every night, Funakoshi walked to his instructor's house and practiced, and then came home in the early hours of the morning.

Azato, his instructor, was an expert in archery, sword fighting, and karate. He was also a brilliant scholar. Azato was a strict teacher, too. Funakoshi would do a kata (a series of prearranged movements, like a martial arts dance) over and over. Azato would only say, "Do it again," or "Use more power." It would take months, even years, of practicing a kata before Azato would say, "Good." Then, and only then, would Azato teach Funakoshi the next kata.

Funakoshi trained very hard. When strong winds and typhoons came, he would climb onto the roof of his house and stand in a horse stance (a common wide stance in Okinawan karate). This helped him develop stability. He practiced for years to perfect a single kata. He would relentlessly punch a *makiwara* board, a rope-covered board for practicing strikes. He also sometimes studied with the great master Bushi Matsumura.

Gradually, karate became more common, and the ban against practicing it was lifted. Funakoshi earned a living as a schoolteacher, but he continued to practice karate every available moment. Karate taught Funakoshi discipline and self-respect, and so he dreamt of giving all people the opportunity to learn those skills. If everyone could learn discipline and self-respect through karate, Funakoshi believed, it could lead to a better world.

Above: Karate masters such as Gichin Funakoshi practice martial arts for countless hours over a period of many years, sometimes an entire lifetime.

In the early 1900s, Funakoshi demonstrated Okinawan martial arts to a Japanese man who was the commissioner of schools. Soon afterward, karate was included in the curriculum for Japanese physical education. In 1921, Funakoshi demonstrated in front of Crown Prince Hirohito (later the emperor of Japan), who was traveling in Okinawa. Funakoshi was instrumental in beginning karate clubs at Japanese universities. He became friends with the founder of judo, Jigoro Kano. Kano persuaded him to stay in Tokyo, where, in 1936, Funakoshi opened up a school for karate. He believed that karate was not just a physical exercise, but could also strengthen the mind and spirit. He believed that the study of karate could make someone a better person— kinder, and more compassionate.

Funakoshi was a humble man, and taught that karate would teach others humility. He once told a story about the Little Man and the True Karate Man: On receiving his first black belt, the Little Man runs home and shouts to everyone about what he has received. When the Little Man gets his second black belt rank, he climbs up to the roof and shouts to the whole neighborhood about his rank. When he receives his third black belt rank, he jumps in his automobile and parades through town, telling everyone about his new rank. When the True Karate Man receives his first black belt, he bows his head in thankfulness. When he gets his second black belt rank, he bows his head and shoulders. When the True Karate Man gets his third black belt rank, he bows at the waist and then quietly walks alongside the wall so that people will not see him or notice him.

Above: A martial artist with a black belt in karate. Gichin Funakoshi believed that karate should teach people to be humble, even when they achieve a high rank.

Above: A pair of karate stylists practice their form, or kata.

Funakoshi taught that kata was the heart of karate. He believed that sparring, practice fighting, and tournaments belittled karate. He knew it would take years to perfect a kata, and so learning it was all that would be required of a karate student. Karate was all about individual self-improvement and learning to respect others.

After World War II, Funakoshi continued his quest to bring karate to the world. He trained American Air Force personnel. He prepared his own students to go out and teach. He founded the style called *shotokan* karate. It is now one of the most popular styles in the world.

Left: Two karate students bow to each other before performing their kata. Bowing is a form of respect for each other and one's self.

One of Funakoshi's principles of karate is that karate begins and ends with the bow, which is a form of respect. More than just an action, the bow is an attitude that pervades all of karate. This means respect not only for each other, but respect for one's self. Any combat that lacks the bow is not a martial art, but merely violence.

GLOSSARY

Belt

Most modern martial arts schools use a system of colored belts to rank their students based on their abilities and length of training. Each school decides the exact order of belts, but most are similar in ranking. A typical school might start beginner students at white belt. From there, the students progress to gold belt, then green, purple, blue, red, and brown. The highest belt is black. It usually takes from three to five years of intense training to achieve a black belt.

Judo

A martial arts style created by Dr. Jigoro Kano in Japan in the late 1800s. The word *judo* means "the gentle way." Dr. Kano believed his martial art was the gentle way to learn about life. Judo stylists use throws, trips, and falls to overpower their opponents.

Kung Fu

A Chinese martial art that had an early influence on the development of other martial arts worldwide, such as karate. The phrase kung fu means "achievement through great effort."

Monk

A person who lives in a religious community. Monks usually take certain vows, such as nonviolence or poverty, to help them focus less on the distractions of the outside world. Buddhist monks from China's Shaolin Temple were some of the first to use kung fu, both as a method of exercise and self-defense, and also as a way to clear the mind.

Okinawa

The birthplace of modern karate. The main island of Okinawa is part of the Ryukyu chain of islands, which are situated in the Pacific Ocean south of Japan. Although it was once an independent nation, Okinawa today is a prefecture, or state, of Japan.

Samurai

The trained warrior class of medieval Japan.

Tournament

A series of contests, usually in a specific sport or game, between a number of competitors. Winners play winners, until only two people are left to compete. The winner of this final competition is the ultimate champion.

World War II

A war that was fought from 1939 to 1945, involving countries around the world. The United States entered the war after Japan's bombing of the American naval base at Pearl Harbor, in Oahu, Hawaii, on December 7, 1941.

Above: A black belt karate master.

INDEX